Ladybird  Readers

The Nutcracker

Series Editor: Sorrel Pitts
Text adapted by Nicole Irving
Activities written by Catrin Morris
Illustrated by Kelly O'Neill

LADYBIRD BOOKS

UK | USA | Canada | Ireland | Australia
India | New Zealand | South Africa

Ladybird Books is part of the Penguin Random House group of companies
whose addresses can be found at global.penguinrandomhouse.com.
www.penguin.co.uk www.puffin.co.uk www.ladybird.co.uk

Penguin
Random House
UK

First published 2020
001

Copyright © Ladybird Books Ltd, 2020

Printed in China

A CIP catalogue record for this book is available from the British Library

ISBN: 978-0-241-40177-4

All correspondence to:
Ladybird Books
Penguin Random House Children's
80 Strand, London WC2R 0RL

MIX
Paper from
responsible sources
FSC® C018179
FSC
www.fsc.org

The Nutcracker

Picture words

Clara

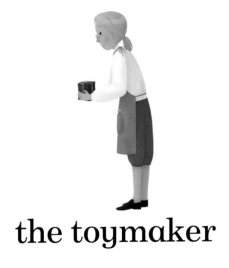

the toymaker

the
Nutcracker

the
Sugarplum
Fairy

Candy Land

dream

present

midnight

sleigh

Christmas

It was Christmas, and there was a party at Clara's house. "Hello!" Clara said to the toymaker.

"Great," she thought.
"My favorite friend is here!"

"Look at our beautiful Christmas tree!" said Clara.

"I made this present for you,"
said the toymaker.
"Thank you," said Clara.

10

After the party, Clara sat with her present under the Christmas tree.

Her eyes were soon closed.

The noise of the clock woke Clara up. It was midnight.

"Oh," she said, "a nutcracker! What a nice present. But why am I so small?"

"Clara, that mouse
wants to catch you!"
said the Nutcracker.

Clara threw a ball of paper at the mouse.

"Well done," said the Nutcracker. "Now, let's go."

The Nutcracker's sleigh flew above the houses and trees.

"Look at the snow," Clara said. "Let's stop and play!"

"It's beautiful. I love snow!"
said Clara.

18

"Are you hungry now?"
the Nutcracker asked.

"Oh, yes!" Clara smiled.

"We can eat in Candy Land," said the Nutcracker. Soon Clara could see many beautiful colors below the sleigh.

"Look," the Nutcracker said. "It's all candy, chocolate, and cake."

"Meet my friend, the Sugarplum Fairy," the Nutcracker said.

"What a nice dress! Is it candy?" Clara asked the fairy.

"Yes, my dress is candy," said the fairy.

"Let's sit and eat," said the Sugarplum Fairy.

They ate lots of candy, chocolate, and cake.

"Would you like an apple?" asked the Sugarplum Fairy.

"Yes, please!" said Clara.

"Now," said the fairy, "let's dance and sing."

They all danced and sang.

"Thank you. We must go home now," said the Nutcracker.

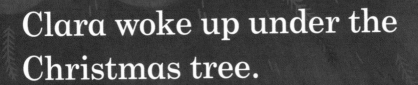

Clara woke up under the Christmas tree.

"Oh, I'm big again," she said. "Was it only a dream?"

Then, she saw the Nutcracker next to her. There was snow under his feet, and he wore a warm coat . . .

Activities

The key below describes the skills practiced in each activity.

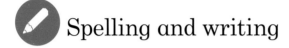 Spelling and writing

 Reading

Speaking

Critical thinking

Preparation for the Cambridge Young Learners exams

1 Match the words to the pictures.

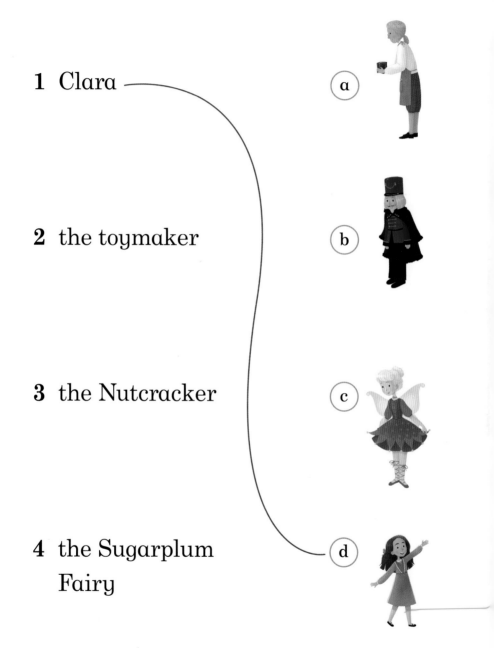

1 Clara

2 the toymaker

3 the Nutcracker

4 the Sugarplum
   Fairy

a

b

c

d

oymouseresnowjsvdreaminsmidnightouernutcrackerswopresentogsleigh

mouse

snow

present

nutcracker

midnight

sleigh

dream

3 Look and read. Choose the correct words and write them on the lines.

the toymaker

the Sugarplum Fairy

Clara

the Nutcracker

1 He makes things for children. _the toymaker_

2 He wears red and gold clothes. ....

3 She can fly. ....

4 She is a little girl. ....

4 Circle the correct pictures.

1 She is Clara's mother.

 a
 b
 c

2 This is Clara's Christmas present.

 a
 b
 c

3 It wants to catch Clara.

 a
 b
 c

4 You can eat this.

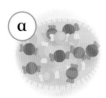 a
 b
 c

5 **Ask and answer the questions with a friend.**

"Look at our beautiful Christmas tree!" said Clara.

"I made this present for you," said the toymaker. "Thank you," said Clara.

1 Who is in the room?

Clara, Clara's mother, and the toymaker.

2 Who does Clara want to look at the tree?

3 What did the toymaker make for Clara?

4 Does Clara like her present?

6 Look, match, and write the words.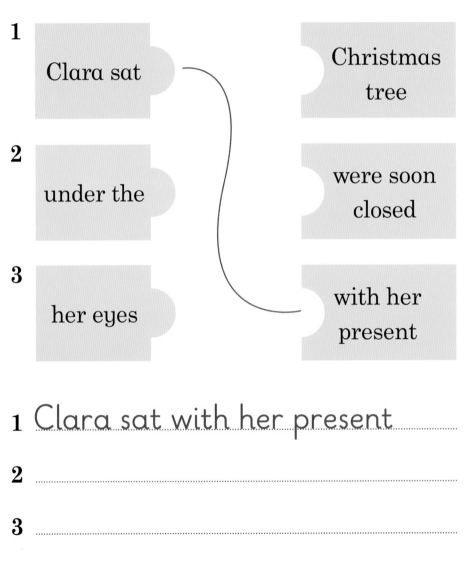

1 Clara sat — Christmas tree

2 under the — were soon closed

3 her eyes — with her present

1 Clara sat with her present

2

3

7 **Write the correct verbs.**

The noise of the clock woke Clara up. It was midnight.

"Oh," she said, "a nutcracker! What a nice present. But why am I so small?"

"Clara, that mouse wants to catch you!" said the Nutcracker.

1 The noise of the clock **(wake)**
___woke___ Clara up.

2 It **(be)** _____ midnight.

3 "Oh," she **(say)** _____,
"a nutcracker!"

4 "What a nice present. But why
(be) _____ I so small?"

5 "Clara, that mouse **(want)**
_____ to catch you!"

8 **Look at the letters. Write the words.** 📖 ✏️ ✦

> d i m g t i h n

1 The noise of the clock woke Clara up. It was ....midnight.....

> r e s p n t e

2 What a nice ....

> o s u e m

3 Clara threw a ball of paper at the

....

> h e g i l s

4 The Nutcracker's .... flew above the houses and trees.

> w o s n

5 "Look at the ....," Clara said. "Let's stop and play!"

38

9 **Look and read. Write the correct words in the boxes.** 📖 ✏️ ❓

Christmas   Candy Land   house

midnight   nutcracker   cake

When?	Where?	What?
Christmas		

10 **Read the questions.**
Write the answers.

1 What does Clara love?

She loves the snow.

2 Is Clara hungry now?

....

3 Where can they eat?

....

4 What can they eat?

....

40

11 Read the text. Choose the correct words, and write them next to 1—4.

1	family	friend	friends
2	dress	hat	skirt
3	ate	are eating	eat
4	apple	banana	carrot

"Meet my ^{1} __friend__, the Sugarplum Fairy," the Nutcracker said.

"What a nice ^{2} _____! Is it candy?" Clara asked the fairy.

"Yes, my dress is candy," said the fairy. "Let's sit and eat."

They ^{3} _____ lots of candy, chocolate, and cake.

"Would you like an ^{4} _____?" asked the Sugarplum Fairy.

12 Put a ✓ by the food in the story. 📖

1 apple	✓	**2** banana	☐
3 bread	☐	**4** burger	☐
5 cake	☐	**6** candy	☐
7 carrot	☐	**8** fries	☐
9 cheese	☐	**10** chicken	☐
11 chocolate	☐	**12** potato	☐
13 egg	☐	**14** ice cream	☐

13 **Circle the correct sentences.**

1

a They all danced and sang.

b They all sat and ate.

2

a There was a party at Clara's house.

b There was a garden at Clara's house.

3

a Clara woke up above the Christmas tree.

b Clara woke up under the Christmas tree.

4

a It was hot, and he wore his T-shirt.

b There was snow under his feet, and he wore a warm coat.

14 **Order the story. Write 1—4.**

___1___ The toymaker makes Clara
a present.

_____ Clara eats and dances in
Candy Land.

_____ Clara wakes up under the
Christmas tree, and she is
big again.

_____ Clara flies on the
Nutcracker's sleigh.

15 Write *beautiful*, *big*, *closed*, *favorite*, or *small*. 📖 ✏️

1 "Great," she thought. "My __favorite__ friend is here!"

2 Clara's eyes were soon _____.

3 "What a nice present. But why am I so _____?"

4 "It's _____. I love snow!" said Clara.

5 "Oh, I'm _____ again," she said. "Was it only a dream?"

16 Do the crossword.

Across

1 . . . tree.

2 The toymaker's present is a . . .

4 There was a . . . at Clara's house.

6 The time was . . .

Down

1 . . . Land

3 "Was it only a . . . ?"

5 They fly in a . . .

17 **Write the correct questions.**

1 (am) (so) (small) (Why) (I) (?)

<u>Why am I so small?</u>

2 (you) (now) (hungry) (Are) (?)

....

3 (candy) (dress) (Is) (your) (?)

....

4 (apple) (like) (you) (Would)

(an) (?)

....

....

5 (a) (it) (dream) (Was) (only) (?)

....

Ladybird Readers

Visit www.ladybirdeducation.co.uk
for more FREE Ladybird Readers resources

✓ Digital edition of every title*

✓ Audio tracks (US/UK)

✓ Answer keys

✓ Lesson plans

✓ Role-plays

✓ Classroom display material

✓ Flashcards

✓ User guides

Register and sign up to the newsletter to receive your FREE classroom resource pack!